The Forgetfuls Give a Wedding

LAWRENCE WEINBERG

Illustrated by PAULA WINTER

SCHOLASTIC BOOK SERVICES

NEW YORK · TORONTO · LONDON · AUCKLAND · SYDNEY · TOKYO

The Forgetful Bears are back—

Mr. and Mrs. Forgetful,

ISBN 0-590-31716-4

Text copyright © 1983 by Lawrence Weinberg. Illustrations copyright © 1983 by Paula Winter. All rights reserved. Published by Scholastic Book Services, a division of Scholastic Inc.

12 11 10 9 8 7 6 5 4 3 2 1   3   3 4 5 6/8

their children,
Sally and Tommy Forgetful,

and, of course, Grandpa Forgetful.

P.S. There are other Forgetfuls, too.
You will meet them in this book.

One day Mr. Forgetful
rushed into his house with a letter.
"I have wonderful news!" he shouted.

"What is it? What is it?" everyone asked.

"Hmmm," said Mr. Forgetful. "I really can't remember."

Little Sally said, "Daddy, what's in that letter?"

"Good thinking," Mr. Forgetful beamed.
And he read the letter aloud.

Dear Uncle and Aunt,

Guess what? I am getting married on Sunday! I can't remember his name just now, but he is the nicest bear in the whole world. I'm sure you will like him.

your loving niece,
Veronica

"We're her closest relatives," said Mrs. Forgetful.

"Wouldn't it be nice if we gave her a wedding?"

"Yes! Yes!" shouted Sally and Tommy.

"Let's call her right away."

All the Forgetfuls rushed to the phone.

"Hello, Veronica?" said Mr. Forgetful.

"We're going to make you the most beautiful wedding.

We'll have it at our house and invite the whole family."

"And I'll make your wedding gown myself, darling,"
said Mrs. Forgetful.

"We'll make the decorations," cried Tommy and Sally.

"And on Sunday morning," Grandpa said,
"I'll go down to the railroad station to meet you."

"So don't worry about a thing," they all shouted together.
"LEAVE EVERYTHING TO THE FORGETFULS!"

The Forgetfuls were very busy all week long.

Mrs. Forgetful bought beautiful white lace.
But she forgot about the wedding gown
and made window curtains instead.

Mr. Forgetful made a wonderful cake.
But he forgot what it was for
and wrote "Happy Birthday" on it.

Tommy and Sally got out paper and crayons.

They made lots of decorations.

But they made them for Halloween!

At last, Sunday came.

Grandpa went to the railroad station.

He got there just as

the train was pulling in.

Veronica got off

and kissed Grandpa hello.

"Here, child," Grandpa said.

"Let me take your heavy suitcase."

Just then the conductor called,

"All aboard! The train is leaving."

"Oh, I'd better hurry,"

said Grandpa.

And he hopped on board.

"So long!" he shouted to Veronica.

"Thanks for coming to see me off."

Veronica had to walk
to the Forgetfuls' house by herself.
Mr. Forgetful answered the door.
"I'm sorry young lady,
but we're not buying anything today.
My niece is coming, and we're very busy."

"But I *am* your niece," Veronica said.

"Oh, in that case, come in," said Mr. Forgetful.
"Guess what everybody! Veronica is here."

Mr. Forgetful rushed into the
kitchen and brought out the cake.
All the Forgetfuls sang,
"Happy birthday to you."

"But it's not my birthday —
it's my wedding day," wailed Veronica.

"So it is," said Mrs. Forgetful.
"Hurry everybody. It's time to get dressed."

"Oh, Aunt, I can't wait to see my wedding gown,"
said Veronica.
"Oh, dear!" exclaimed Mrs. Forgetful.
"I knew there was something I forgot to do."
"Now I have nothing to wear," sobbed Veronica.

"Don't cry," said Mrs. Forgetful.
"I have just the thing." She took down her lace curtains
and pinned them on Veronica.

"There, now," she said. "They look much lovelier
on you than they did on the windows."

Just then Mr. Forgetful called,
"Hurry up. It's time to go to the church."

All the Forgetfuls rushed to the car.

"Which church are we going to, Uncle?" asked Veronica.

"Hmmm," said Mr. Forgetful.

"It seems to have slipped my mind.

"We'll just look for the one with the wedding in it."

They drove and they drove,

but they couldn't find the right church.

"Am I going to miss my very own wedding?"
Veronica asked in a tiny voice.
"Not a chance," said Mr. Forgetful.
"Not as long as our name is . . . er . . . er . . ."

Just then they heard the sound of organ music.
It was coming from the last church in town.

Mr. Forgetful stopped the car.

"Run," he shouted. "They're starting without us."

Veronica ran so fast her veil fell down over her face.

She could hardly see.

Mr. Forgetful grabbed her by the arm

and rushed her down the aisle.

"Hold everything!" he called. "The bride is here."

The groom was waiting at the altar.
Mr. Forgetful took one look at him
and whispered to his wife,
"She's marrying the ugliest bear I've ever seen."

The groom's mother heard what he said.
It made her very angry.
"My son may be ugly looking for a bear," she yelled.
"But for a *giraffe*, he is just right."

Veronica pulled back her veil and stared.
"He's the WRONG ONE!" she cried.
Her uncle scratched his head.
"Are you sure, Veronica?
Remember, you *are* a Forgetful."

"He's the WRONG ONE!"

"At least he's nice and tall, dear,"
said Mrs. Forgetful.

"I am marrying *my* bear," Veronica shouted,
"not *that* giraffe!"
She burst into tears and ran out of the church.

The Forgetfuls raced after her.

"Don't cry, Veronica. We'll find your wedding."

"Why did you change everything?" asked Veronica.

"You said it was going to be at your house."

"Our house?" said Mrs. Forgetful.

"What a wonderful idea!"

"Let's go!" cried Mr. Forgetful.

And they all jumped into the car.

They arrived at the house in no time.

But the door was locked.

No one had any keys.

"Well," Mrs. Forgetful said, "there's one thing
I do remember. And that is how to climb a tree."

So up the tree she went
and climbed through a window.
Then she ran downstairs and let everyone in.

Mr. Forgetful looked around.

"Something funny is going on," he said.

"Yes," agreed Tommy. "All the furniture has been changed."

"Yes," said Sally. "The rooms are not in the same place."

Veronica tugged at Mr. Forgetful's sleeve.

"Uncle," she whispered. "I have to tell you something."

"What?" asked Mr. Forgetful.

"THIS IS THE WRONG HOUSE!"

"It certainly is," said Mrs. Forgetful.

"I think that wallpaper is dreadful."

Just then a police officer
came through the door.
"Don't move, you crooks!" he ordered.
"You're all under arrest. Put up your paws."

"Why it's my cousin, Officer Forgetful.
What a wonderful surprise!" said Mr. Forgetful.
"Maybe you can help us find our house?"
"That's what cousins are for," said Officer Forgetful.
"Your troubles are over. Just follow my motorcycle."

"On the other hand," he said as they went outside,
"where *is* my motorcycle?
Oh, well, never mind. I'll just sit here on the
hood and point the way."

At last, the Forgetfuls were home.

All the guests were waiting on the porch.

"Hooray!" they shouted. "Here comes the bride."

Reverend Forgetful was there, too.

"Let's get started with the wedding ceremony

before I forget how to do it," he said.

"Where is the lucky groom?"

"The groom. THE GROOM!!" Veronica screamed.

"Oh, NO! I forgot to tell him where to meet us."

And she fainted dead away.

"Perhaps I should go back and get the giraffe,"

Mr. Forgetful suggested.

All at once they heard the honk of a horn.

A taxi pulled up in front of the house.

Two bears got out.

One of them was Grandpa.

"I'm back!" Grandpa said proudly.

"See? I remembered the wedding.

And I met this nice young fellow on the train.

He was trying to get to a wedding, too.

But he didn't know where it was.

So I brought him along."

Veronica opened her eyes and stared.

"It's Charlie!" she cried.

She rushed into his arms.

"My darling, you look lovely," said Charlie.

"But what is *that* sticking out of your dress?"

"Oh, dear!" said Mrs. Forgetful.

"I forgot to take out the curtain rod."

The marriage ceremony began.

"Veronica and Charlie," said Reverend Forgetful.

"Do you want to get married?"

"I do," said Veronica.

"I do, too," said Charlie.

"Good," said the Reverend. "Now put the ring on her finger."

Charlie looked in one pocket and then another.

"I can't believe it," he cried.

"I forgot to bring the ring."

"WELCOME TO THE FORGETFUL FAMILY!"
everybody shouted.

Then they all kissed and cheered and sang and danced and had a wonderful time — which they never forgot.